The Police Station

Julie Murray

Abdo
Kids
MY COMMUNITY: PLACES

abdopublishing.com

Published by Abdo Kids, a division of ABDO, PO Box 398166, Minneapolis, Minnesota 55439.
Copyright © 2017 by Abdo Consulting Group, Inc. International copyrights reserved in all countries.
No part of this book may be reproduced in any form without written permission from the publisher.

Printed in the United States of America, North Mankato, Minnesota.

052016

092016

THIS BOOK CONTAINS
RECYCLED MATERIALS

Photo Credits: Alamy, Glow Images, iStock, Shutterstock,
©Abdul Sami Haqqani p.19, ©meunierd p.21 / Shutterstock.com

Production Contributors: Teddy Borth, Jennie Forsberg, Grace Hansen

Design Contributors: Christina Doffing, Candice Keimig, Dorothy Toth

Cataloging-in-Publication Data

Names: Murray, Julie, author.

Title: The police station / by Julie Murray.

Description: Minneapolis, MN : Abdo Kids, [2017] | Series: My community: places
    | Includes bibliographical references and index.

Identifiers: LCCN 2015959207 | ISBN 9781680805383 (lib. bdg.) |
    ISBN 9781680805949 (ebook) | ISBN 9781680806502 (Read-to-me ebook)

Subjects: LCSH: Police stations--Juvenile literature. | Buildings--Juvenile
    literature.

Classification: DDC 363.2--dc23

LC record available at http://lccn.loc.gov/2015959207

Table of Contents

The Police Station

Mark is a police officer.

He works at the police station.

The station has meeting rooms. Bill does roll call.

Amy works in the call center.

She takes calls for help.

9

Fingerprints are taken.

Sara helps.

There are holding cells.

Suspects are kept here.

There is a break room.

Mal eats lunch.

Police **equipment** is here.

Ana puts on her vest.

16

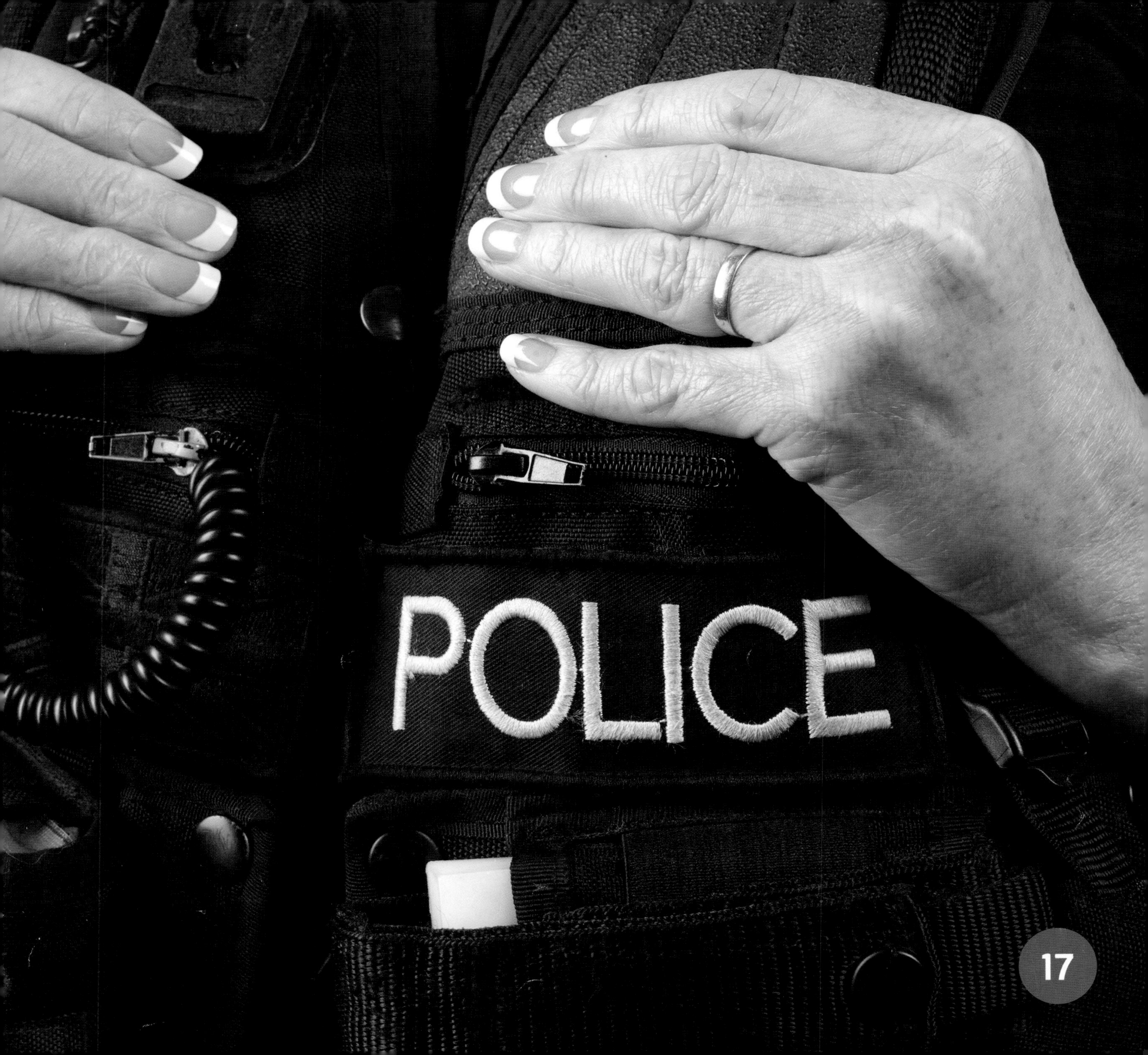
POLICE

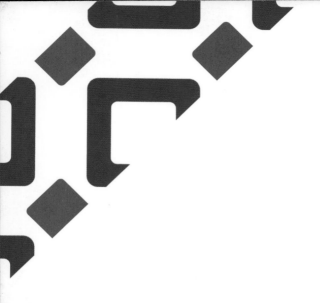

Police cars park here.

They are ready to go!

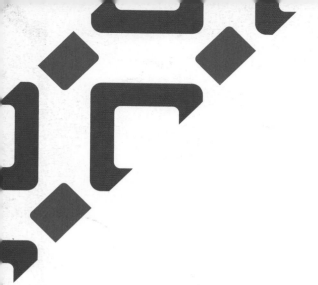

Have you been to a police station?

21

At the Police Station

fingerprint

police car

holding cell

police gear

Glossary

equipment
tools, clothing, and other things
needed to do something.

fingerprint
an ink mark made by a
person's fingertip.

suspect
a person thought to be guilty
of a crime.

Index

abdokids.com

Use this code to log on to abdokids.com and access crafts, games, videos, and more!

Abdo Kids Code:
MTK5383